ELEPHANT PIE

Hilda Offen

Hamish Hamilton • London

For Steve and Julie

HAMISH HAMILTON LTD

Published by the Penguin Group
27 Wrights Lane, London W8 5TZ, England
Penguin Books USA Inc, 375 Hudson Street, New York, New York 10014, USA
Penguin Books Australia Ltd, Ringwood, Victoria, Australia
Penguin Books Canada Ltd, 10 Alcorn Avenue, Toronto, Ontario, Canada M4V 3B2
Penguin Books (NZ) Ltd, 182-190 Wairau Road, Auckland 10, New Zealand

Penguin Books Ltd, Registered Offices: Harmondsworth, Middlesex, England

First Published in Great Britain 1993 by Hamish Hamilton Ltd

Text and illustrations copyright © 1993 by Hilda Offen

1   3   5   7   9   10   8   6   4   2

British Library Cataloguing in Publication Data
CIP data for this book is available from the British Library

ISBN 0-241-13269-X

Printed in Hong Kong by Imago Publishing

"What would you like for your birthday, my dearest dear?" asked Mr Snipper-Snapper.

"A party!" said Mrs Snipper-Snapper. "And a cherry pie – with lots and lots of custard!" She was so excited that she burst into tears. The Snipper-Snappers were a very weepy family.

Splish! Splash! Mr Snipper-Snapper ran to fetch the mop. Then he looked up "Pies" in the telephone book.

Ting-a-ling-a-ling! Mrs Elephant answered the phone. "The Snipper-Snappers want a birthday pie!" she told her children.

"Please let me help!" said Edward.

"No, Edward!" said his mother. "You muddle things up. Last time you put pepper in the pastry."

Mrs Elephant fetched a bowl of cherries from the larder.

"Want some!" said baby Jojo.

"Not now, Jojo!" said Mrs Elephant. "Go and play with your building bricks."

Mrs Elephant rolled the pastry. She made the pie in her biggest dish and popped it in the oven.

When the pie was cooked, Mrs Elephant set it on the table to cool. Then she iced it and decorated it with candles and marzipan roses. "Now for the washing," said Mrs Elephant. "You can help me if you like, Edward."

But when they came back, Jojo had disappeared.

Naughty Jojo! Where could she be? They looked in the cupboards – no Jojo.

They looked under the beds – no Jojo.

They looked in the laundry basket – no Jojo.
Mrs Elephant was frantic!

"Oh dear, could Jojo have gone out of the gate again?"
she cried. "Oh dear – Edward, you'll have to deliver
the pie! Oh dear, oh dear, I mustn't forget the custard!"

But Mrs Elephant was so flustered
She muddled the mustard with the custard.
She made the custard out of mustard!

"Mum!" said Edward. "You've made a mistake!"

Mrs Elephant was too hot and bothered to listen. She loaded the pie into the wheelbarrow and put the custard into Edward's rucksack. "Keep a look out for your sister!" she said. Then she ran off up the lane calling, "Jojo! Jojo!"

Edward set off with the wheelbarrow. "Jojo!" he called. "Where are you?"

"We've seen her up that pine tree!"
shrieked some parrots. Edward went to
look. While he was gone the parrots
pecked all the candles off the pie.
Then they flew away.

"Jojo!" called Edward as he went through the wood.
A bear ran out from amongst the trees.

"I've seen her near the pond," it said.

Edward went to look. While he was gone the bear ate
all the marzipan roses. Then it ran away.

Edward came to a field. "Jojo!" he called. A donkey
leaned over the hedge.

"I've seen her in that ditch!" it said.

Edward went to look.

While he was gone the donkey nibbled away most of the pie-frill. Then it galloped off.

The pie looked dreadful. "Perhaps the Snipper-Snappers won't notice," said Edward to himself. He trundled the wheelbarrow up to their front door and knocked.

Mr Snipper-Snapper opened the door.

"Your pie!" said Edward.

Mr Snipper-Snapper stared.
Mrs Snipper-Snapper stared.
The Aunties and the Uncles and all the little Snipper-Snappers stared.

"This?" cried Mrs Snipper-Snapper.
"*This* is my birthday pie?"

She began to sob. Her tears splashed onto the doorstep and trickled away down the path.

Mr Snipper-Snapper snatched the pie and slammed the door in Edward's face.

"Boo-hoo!" sobbed Mrs Snipper-Snapper. "Boo-hoo!" wailed the Aunties and Uncles. "Boo-hoo!" roared the little Snipper-Snappers. What a row! Jojo opened one eye. She had eaten all the cherries and had fallen fast asleep. Now she yawned. She stretched. The pie-crust began to crack!

"Oh!" gasped the Snipper-Snappers as Jojo burst out of the pie.

"Wah!" screamed Jojo. "I want my mum!"

When Edward heard his sister's voice he ran and
peeped through the window. And what did he see?
He saw Jojo sitting in the pie-dish! And he saw the
Snipper-Snappers crowding round and clicking their
terrible teeth.

"Never mind the cherries, my dear!" he heard Mr Snipper-Snapper say. "We'll have Elephant Pie instead."

"Oh dear!" thought Edward. "What shall I do?" Then he had an idea. "Don't you want your custard?" he called.

"The custard! The custard!" squealed the Snipper-Snappers. Mrs Snipper-Snapper snatched the jug and tipped it over Jojo's head. Slippety-slop! Down poured the custard, over Jojo's ears, over her tummy and into the pie-dish.

"Mm!" said Mrs Snipper-Snapper. "I love custard!"

She leaned forward and took a big sip. All the other Snipper-Snappers did the same.

"Aargh!" they shrieked as the mustard in the custard burned their tongues.

Tears sprang to the Snipper-Snappers' eyes and poured to the floor. Soon they were knee-deep in water. "Boo-hoo!" they howled. "Boo-hoo!" Their tongues were on fire! The more they cried the higher the water rose. It reached the table-top — and away floated Jojo on the pie-dish, across the room and out of the window!

Edward put her in the wheelbarrow and ran. He ran and he ran and he didn't stop running until he reached home.

Mrs Elephant was overjoyed to see her baby safe and sound.

"Well done, Edward!" she said.

She gave Jojo a bath and washed off all the mustard custard. Then she tucked her into bed.

But she let Edward stay up late. And she let him make a pie, a pie of his very own. It was a strawberry pie, with cream on the top, and they had it for supper.

"It's a perfect pie!" said Mrs Elephant.
"It's the best pie I've ever tasted!"